In the Name of Love
AF506519

In the Name of Love

The Poems of a Hopelessly Hopeless Romantic

Matthew M Smerglia

Big Bets Media and Publishing, LLC

Dedicated first and foremost to my family and closest friends. I love you all so much and cannot be more grateful you are in my life and who I get to be surrounded by daily.

Also dedicated to anyone I have ever crossed paths with; to both those that have believed in me and to those that have doubted me.

At the end of the day, I am who I am in part because of interactions and moments I have shared with each and every one of you and for that, I am thankful. I am following a passion and ultimately I hope you are too. Much love.

Last but certainly not least, a HUGE special dedication and thank you to **Sara Noakes** *who thoughtfully answered any questions I had and took the time to help me edit and prepare this book for publishing. I am forever appreciative of how sweet you always are when I reach out and for all your help! I can't wait to see all of the success and happiness you find as you follow your passions and chase your dreams!*

Table of Contents

2015

Guarded

Staring through a brick wall

Is nearly impossible;

Yet I continue to try and call

To wake up your sense, if possible.

I'm trying to beat it down,

But nothing works,

And it feels like I may drown

In your eyes and in your skirt.

However, closed eyes don't see

And hushed lips don't speak,

What we need to be

Is strong and not so weak.

Let your senses be alive;

Your future may be now, we can thrive.

Love and Death

Love and Death,

Is one not the other

I think as I draw my final breath

Knowing there will never be another.

Oh the wedding is great,

Though I can't help but to think

Of when we will build our wall of hate,

The one that will push past the brink.

My love ran deep

But turned cold quick

As a dark feeling began to creep

Into my head, making me sick.

Love is like no other

But I realized more

While there isn't another

Death means amor.

I'm agreeing to serve life

For love that proves

It brings out strife

Whenever I move.

A wedding is a funeral

Dressed in white,

Making it more cruel

Yet less of a fright.

But what becomes so great,

Life is full of surprises

And on any given date

Rebirth is found when one dies.

So I snapped to reality

And saw the blue-eyed beauty

That would save me, maybe

If I revoked my duty.

With love, life lives on

But death becomes more real

With each passing dawn

Yet more life I will steal.

Death is love's finale

But love is death's glory

And now I know finally

The end of the story.

Foolishly Lost

Lost is a man who knows too much.

He feels far back and observational

Yet he's right in the moment yearning for more.

Confused and distracted his mind never rests.

A heart can open too much

And distribute too much love.

A fool is a man who loves too much

And wow am I a fool.

Right there in front of me I always see

But I hide behind the blackness of my eyelids

Blinking away the thought

But never getting rid of the idea.

Inspired I may be

But motivated I may not be,

Lost is accurate

Foolish and scared too.

I see an attainable life

And a life I want to have,

Sometimes they merge

But other times they migrate.

It can be so easy to see

Though, it's easier to deceive.

And this is where perception shatters

And the glass begins to cut.

Reality is a theory

About having a theory in reality

And sometimes we disconnect from reality

Following a different theory.

We only pick one road, however,

It often being the weakest one.

Take a risk,

Just leap.

Leap, and take me with you,

Carry me beyond.

I want to know more,

I want to get more lost.

Let theory and reality become one in the same

Explore a different path,

I will always have faith

If you pull me off the cliff.

You won't see me waver,

For I am foolish and stubborn,

But I want more

And more is hard to describe.

Beauty is found in many forms,

Forms where words cannot capture it.

I yearn for such beauty

And sometimes I know it's always close by.

Sometimes I give distance,

Sometimes I can't get enough.

A lost soul is foolish, which tempts my desires

Because I have never had enough.

Struggling to See

Your love is poisoned;

It's just hate bathed in red.

Your love is bleeding,

Not sterling hearts.

A pain you don't feel

Kills you everyday,

Silently working through you

Eradicating all logic.

Your head is clouded;

Your heart sick;

Listen now to your gut

For it's not what you're doing.

It is screaming stop,

Pleading for someone to call 911.

It says get help,

While you still can that is.

In front of you

Is a figure standing

Waiting to save you

But you're standing there blind.

Reach out and feel

So that you can really see

You should put faith in that figure

And let them in.

Your path has changed

Assuredly for the better,

Just step into the light

And begin anew.

2016

A Better Future

I'm better off now

Than I was back then

My mind is all fucked up

But I don't care

The past is the past

And the future is now

We make history every second

So don't let me down.

Excerpts from my short story, **<u>Running Away from the Sunset</u>**

Voices

Left foot, right foot. Left foot, right foot. Wipe away tear. Ignore voices. *Left foot, right foot.* Find car. Car door. Car handle. Gone.

Aghast

Lying awake I'm noticing the ceiling for the first time.

I stare, my eyes tracing outlines of anything my mind pretends it sees above, as if I were laying outside on a sunny day watching the clouds.

A golf club, a sword, a nutty professor.

I must be crazy.

Empty.

How'd I get here?

RAFTS

"Aren't we all just running away from a sunset? That's what life is. It's just one long ass day."

She let out a nervous cackle.

"The sun rises and we're born, filled with hope. We go through life and we embrace the sunshine; we brave the storms; we marvel at the rainbows. But then one day, for all of us, the sun sets."

I tried to watch the sunset the best I could in my passenger side window, ears at attention to her words.

"Life ends and our world becomes the darkness we sleep in. So, we run and we run and we run, all our lives, like we can avoid something so natural. Nature doesn't stop for us. Time doesn't stop for us. We run with the earth as it turns, except the earth keeps turning once we've been rolled into our graves."

In the mirror, I watched Annalise and I running together down the road, back towards the sunset.

"Your life is your odyssey. It's how you live your one long ass day on this planet. Until you finally stop running, that is. Everyone watches the sunset wash over them then."

2017

Cyclical

I'm sorry, doll

That I can't be all that you expect of me,

But take comfort knowing after they fall

A Phoenix rises anew, free.

An enigma so blinding,

Rushing past at the speed of light,

Has left you finding

You don't see the vision, only the sight.

A path formerly correct

Now lies dormant,

Lost in the stars and unable to detect

That now past is the special moment.

Not all is lost,

As time speeds ahead

And more stars cross,

A new moment wishes to take you to bed.

The Good, the Bad, and the Ugly

It's a shame to see the ugly in this world

Grow and grow and grow,

But why has that ugliness captivated us so?

When did ugly gain so much power,

That it can turn us away from all the beauty?

For all of eternity

There has been light versus dark,

Mankind knows no earlier battle

Than good versus evil,

So why now shy away from the beauty we still see?

We as humans are creators,

Of the good, the bad, and the ugly.

We have a chance to paint a portrait

With the entire world our canvas,

We can be the creators of beauty

We need only the vision.

Stop seeing the ugly in the world and staring,

Use that vision and put it into action.

It's true we can bring back beauty in this world,

But it must be done together.

Your Escape

How can I be your escape

When I'm trapped?

When I'm stuck searching

Just the same as you

For meaning

For happiness

You look to me

But I look to the sky

And ask nothing else save, why?

I want to be your way out

The door to everything better in life

But how can that happen yet?

My head is screwed on backwards

I'm looking the wrong way

Though you may beg and plead

I can only hope to finally forge our path

And find our escape.

Standstill

Passively living

An active life

Watching others

Realize dreams

While I stay,

Dreaming.

Transfixed

Right across the table

You sit,

Glasses fixed,

And I'm not sure just how I'm able

To ease my mind,

Erase the fear,

And emerge in the clear

Freed from your bind.

Your gaze,

A lock to which I have no key,

Entices me, denies me,

Knocks me into a haze.

I know not how to act,

Stricken by paralysis

Making it hard to persist,

A comment hangs in the air I wish to redact.

No, push forward!

I must insist...

Refuse to resist...

But I look up and I see you coming toward

Closer and closer,

There are sparks dancing on your lips,

And my breath comes in sips

Moving in slow motion like a stoner.

The air between us finally evaporates,

Heated up past its boiling point

With no time to disappoint,

No time to debate.

Fraud

I wear a cape

To look like a hero

But to feel like anyone but me

I stare out the window

At the sunny sky

But I see gray clouds,

Rain pouring down

And it is hard to feel proud

The storms keep coming

My head keeps pounding

The self doubt has been crippling

Since its founding

Will it last

Or will it pass

Nobody will know its existence

But for now, we're at an impasse.

Your Power

There's power in the crowd

But it's your voice that's so loud

Ringing in my head

It's the reason I can't get out of bed

Time with you is all I seek

Into our future I have already peeked

There's no part of me that doesn't believe

If we got together we would never leave

When you walk in a room

All else melts away and we're in a vacuum

I only see you

Even when I don't want to

But in the end that is fine by me

Because with you is when I actually feel free.

2019

My Pledge

I swear my fealty

To none other before thee

For nothing else matters

Lest I get to be by your side

It is your happiness I care for

Above all else

You are my sun and my moon

My stars, my galaxy and my universe

You complete me in a way nothing else in this life can

And I will never take that for granted

Instead, I will serve and worship

Building a life we love and are proud of

And do anything to see your sweet smile

Grace your face, for the rest of my days.

Rinse and Repeat

The pain I manifest

Is the pain I cleanse

As I rinse and repeat

Opening old wounds nightly

With thoughts like a revolving door

Never finding their right resolution

I wish I could burn the paperwork

And just forget.

Contemplation

At a glance

He stands alone

Both wondering and wishing

In the same moment…

Can I do this?

The Present

You never know what's coming next

So enjoy what is in front of you right now.

By the Tracks

A mind filled with ghosts of the past

And dreams of better days in the future,

But a body stuck living in the present

Standing at the edge of the train tracks

Nearly struck time after time

They whiz by, but I'm unscathed

I'm a doubt filled being

A creature of habit searching for meaning

Yearning for a future I'm scared to create

I can see it but am scared to leap across the tracks

I want it but how do I take the first step?

Not Deterred

I wish that I could say I'm proud,

I'm sorry that I let you down

All these voices in my head get loud

I wish that I could shut them out

But I have to push forward

The best that I can

To keep moving toward

The life I showed us

It's still achievable

If you will allow me the chance.

In Love

Your hair flips

You flash your smile

Turning away from me as you go

I can capture the moment

Slow it down

Replay it

Savor it.

My feet walk

But my heart dances

My spirit flies

And my thoughts race

An obstacle course

That we used to navigate

Is soon to be a crash course.

The sun shines down

Illuminating the way forward

And darkening the past

So a new union may form

A strengthening bond

Here we are again

Face to face.

Your eyes glitter

Like a diamond

Your hand ruffles my hair

We laugh into each other

Knowing what was long overdue

We can now proceed

Let the passion whirl.

Mind in Battle

It's all just another memory

Of a time that wasn't meant to be

As I lay in my bed

These thoughts racing through my head

To remind me such dreams do exist

And I must persist

But how many missed opportunities

And false unities

Can pass me by

Before I stop telling myself those lies.

Swing Away

In my dreams we're always okay

But that's just it

It's in my head where you stay

Oh I know I'm the culprit

And that doesn't change today

But after all the shit

There has to be something to say

For not forgetting the way we hit.

The Tank

It's not like that at all

Don't misconstrue words on a page

For writing on the wall

We've moved off the stage

Phones silent, no calls

I've been locked in a cage

While you play with my voodoo doll

But there's still some gas in our gauge.

Cardiac Arrest

Cardiac arrest

Stealing your breath from the rest

Whisper to me now

That you can't imagine how

This could be happening again

Things shouldn't be how they've been

But then the moment turns

Because some flames always burn

Take the old and mix it with time

If it's better then it's no crime.

Leader of What

You put a crown on my head

Pushed me though I wasn't ready

Said sink or swim

Then left me high and dry

To figure it out

Or flounder

But after all the hard work

To stay afloat

What is there to even take hold of?

What in front of me isn't a fabrication?

You led me astray

When you wanted to make me a leader

There's nothing here

No one

I am alone

I am a leader of what?

Something New

And so you learn that sometimes

Life is in a hurry,

But it's not a crime

To try and savor the flurry

Of something new

Capture the moments

That will lead you to the next clue

To fix what was broken

You can swim faster yet

Towards what at first may seem scary

But the closer you get to what's next,

The more you want to marry

The future you see

Through sparkling eyes

You can smile now and let it be,

What you want is here so enjoy the ride.

Head First

There's been a shift,

An underlying theme

Has presented itself

In our lives.

A weight so heavy we can't lift,

But as pointless as it seems

I won't stay on the shelf,

Tired of being stabbed with knives.

Through the thick and thin we must sift

Until our reality matches our dreams

Acting thusly as proof to oneself

Why nothing has been contrived.

This life can be a gift,

I'm the cherry to top your whipped cream

If we just trust ourselves,

Hand in hand when we take our dives.

Paralyzed

The right words never seem

To escape my lips

Like a form of paralysis,

I'm stuck in a perpetual dream.

In reality I exist

To pick the worst time

To commit the smallest crime

Of saying you are what I've missed.

In my head it was never wrong

To feel this way

After telling myself a thousand times a day

We were a hit like a number one song.

Living in a haze

The world keeps passing by

But I'm stuck standing still like I'm ready to die

When really I'm just dreaming about the days;

The days I thought I'd have forever

When I thought I was right

But through this eternal fight

It seems I deserve that never.

Masked

Masked when I had you

Now exposed and crumbling

Falling apart at the seams

It seems

I could be off the rails

You kept my mind clear

Motivated me to grow

But now I've sunk and feel low

I don't, I shouldn't need your mask

The facade you help create

But I miss it,

I do.

2020

Watermelon

Blissful summer eve,

A blanket spread along the ground

You roll up your sleeves

For today's work is done and the air is sound.

We can relax

Open the basket

And inside find summers best snack

A refreshing taste, no need to mask it

Our seeds of love

Grow and replace the treat's original seeds

Too happy to share in the fruit we have beloved

For a perfect summers eve that's all we need.

Glass

I'm made of glass

Held together by glue

Little did I know

That the glue was you

Now the cracks are back

And I'm, falling apart

Where did you go?

Lost and unable to start

With no sense of direction

Wandering, wondering

Begging to not be aimless

And finally, here you come in thundering

Careful that I'm fragile

Even with limited time

But you're confident, you're right

Giving me purpose isn't a crime

To you I'll walk, run, crawl

The fix for me is to give you it all.

You in My Arms

Whenever there's a down

Fall back into my arms

Where you'll always wear a crown

Jewels for eyes that I could never harm

We can speak in silence

Nights like these have re-found their charm

You and me equals perfect balance

Out with the inhibitions, we can disarm

We can open ourselves and fly free

Falling into something praying there's no alarm

That will wake us without you by me

Time never stops but I ask that it please slows, with you in my arms.

Skyward

The stars in the sky

Reflect in the twinkle of your eye

In a moment yet to pass,

A moment that can never last

For as long as I wish

Must be careful not to miss

Opportunities are precious

Few will leave you breathless

But when my daydreams and reality blur

I find a common denominator,

You're the cure.

The sun in the sky

Illuminates the oceans in my eyes

You feel the waves crashing

In a moment that's finally happening

The air is still and calm

Matching minds, matching sweaty palms

Nervously hoping this is it

Surely fate makes puzzle pieces that fit

Well when your eyes meet mine

You won't even need a sign

You'll just know, we'll always be more than fine.

No matter what is in the sky,

We can feel safe when we lock eyes

Time likes to not be kind

Plus our sparks?, Makes patience hard to find

Yet so far each moment has been a gift

And the moments to come will finally uplift

Us from where we've been before

To heights too high to see a floor

Maybe it's crazy to think

That we are our missing links

But it'd be crazier to ignore that without each

other maybe we would just sink.

Snowfall // Fallen for You

YELLOW rays shining through

Cast away the dark

The first snowfall replaces the dew

Look at its beauty, hitting its mark

The first snow falls and you don't know if it'll stick

But each unique flake holds its own

Sparkling with hope it gives your heart a kick

Before you know it the amount has grown.

OFFERING no regard for the time of year

Now it's a blistering flurry

Swirling all around, blinding, it could cause a fear

But snow knows no hurry

And all it takes is a moment to pause,

See how a blanket of snow envelops the ground

The moments have built, you can pinpoint the cause

Of the strong foundation you see all around.

UNRELENTING the snow falls and falls

Until it avalanches and hits all at once

It brings down all your walls

But this isn't similar to normal cold fronts

You're quickly filled with a glow, a warmth

As you look out, snow glistening as far as the eye can
see and now you have a clue

This unmatched beauty, you cannot live without it
henceforth

This way the snow falls, is how I fall for... YOU.

Lost Girl, Lost Boy

There she lay

Hair strewn about

Staring at the ceiling

Never filled more with doubt

There he stands

Just outside the door

Hand through his hair

Wondering, thinking there must be more

She sits up quick

Looks to the window

Then to the floor

Struggling to remember their intro

The stories he's told

Of dreams long held

Never seemed so useless

As their souls it did not help weld.

Should she move

Or should she wait?

She stayed frozen

In fear and ill-conceived hate.

Should he go back

Or should he give up?

He knows what to do but it is tough

And instead he just left, a sad little pup.

Hello, Hello

Open the door

And there you are

Hello, hello

We have tonight

There's nothing else

But you and I

Melt away

In each other's eyes

Come here closer

Let me hold you tight

Don't let go

Because it feels so right

A soft kiss here

One more there

Pull away

With a blush and a smile

Tasting so sweet

Foreheads come together

We feel totally at peace

Fingers interlocking

Hand in hand

Time has decided to take it slow

The earths rotation

Temporarily exposed

So we can hold onto this moment

Ever more.

Pleading

A magical touch

Butchered and cut

Call me a fool

It's not cruel

I stay in my own way

To jeopardize the good days

In one fell swoop

But I can recoup

Meaning well

Can't you tell

A few moment's lapse

Shouldn't prevent the dance

We share a bond

Two fish in the same pond

Coming closer together

Any storm we can weather

There are some walls

But none too tall

Patience is our climb

To a peak that is sublime

Trust can be hard

Sometimes you play the wrong card

But if you just trust

I can shake off the rust

A new tale can be written

A new kind of smitten

You never knew

You could feel anew

But here we stand

On fresh land

Ready to embark

Through the light and the dark

On a trip

Where there's no tips

Each path is different

Not sure what it meant

When all seemed lost

When pain seemed to be the cost

But that's a concern no longer

Together we can be stronger

Maintain faith

That you can bury any wraith

Because there's not another me

That will show you how the world should be.

A Perfect Fit

The birds are singing their songs

The sunny skies have moved in

This day was coming all along

We can finally chalk up a win

There's always bound to be turbulence

But then it steadies

With us there's a certain artfulness

Gone through the worst so we're ready

To take hold of what's next

Take our time

And ensure it's the best

That surely can't be a crime

The world feels renewed

Popping with color

You feel it when I feel it too

Kudos to what we discover

You never know what's in store

It's hard to shake feelings of the past

But deep down in your core

You know something new's bound to last

When it is borne of truth

And done right

It hasn't only soothed

But it has brightened the light

Your eyes have a rare shine

To go with a smile that radiates

I hope you enjoy the heart that is mine

And that you may find I captivate

You from head to toe

To your heart and your soul

Like a flower blooms and grows

No need to pay a toll.

Again and Again

Brokenhearted

Hard to restart it

I know that I have to

But it's hard to not ask how

Wish I could ask you why

Though you won't stop the next

From getting my all

Even if my all

Won't stop them

From doing what you did

I know that

Yet I will never change

The heart may be fragile

But I know what it wants

And I will piece it back together

Again and again.

End of the Road

There lies below

No further hope

Time won't slow

And it's hard to cope

One day I'll be without you

By choice or not

Why must that be true?

It puts my stomach in knots

Can't we stay right here

And never move?

You are my peace and I can see clear

It's just one thing after another to prove

How undeniable we are

But that only matters for so long

And suddenly you feel so far

How long will we be this strong?

Slowing Time

Seeing your gaze

Leaves me in a daze

Like time can slow

With nowhere for us to go

I can't help but admire

This strong new desire

As I see your beauty

And hope I have a new duty

To make you smile,

To make you stay awhile.

Forever Hoping

Slave to the potential

And falling short

Try to break me down

But I already have

A shell of myself

And what I could be

Dreaming of glory

But stagnant in mud

A racing mind

Matched by frozen feet

Or, so it seems

It isn't last call

Never too late

There's always hope yet.

Refreshed

Don't mind if I stare

I'm just breathing in a whole new air

And I have to capture this

This, pure bliss

That you make me feel

That can help my soul heal

I don't know where you came from

But my heart is beating like a drum

And I'm blessed

Finally, feeling refreshed

You walk radiating with sparks

Sure to leave your mark

And I'll do my damnedest to keep up

Because once you have my love it doesn't letup.

Down

Soft spoken

And eyes to the floor

Confidence shot

Not sure just how much more

He could take

He was low

Not sure he could fall

Much further below.

Umbrella Love

The world is crashing all around us

But we hadn't even noticed,

An umbrella of love

Providing protection in the storm

And keeping us safe

All I see,

All I need,

Is you.

2021

Big Bang

At the start of the universe

There was nothing

Then suddenly, a Big Bang

An explosion that bore all we know

And trillions of little things all went right

To lead me to you.

I had started feeling nothing

I lost most of my faith

Then suddenly, a Big Bang

I met you and there was an explosion that bore a rush
of emotions

A hundred little new things that were all I ever hoped
for

Thank you universe for leading me to you.

Tidal Love

Like streams to the ocean

We flow together to form something stronger

Large and vast is our love

Powerful, coming in towering waves

And we have an electric chemistry

That can shift the tides in any battle.

Side Effects

Love's cruel side effect

Is love drives the pain

When you feel so strongly

You can't help but struggle and hurt

It may be the smallest thing

But it can cut like a thousand knives

Sometimes there's nothing you can do

Other times you can't do enough

You are along for the ride

Good and bad

Finding true love is life's greatest glory

But beware of the torturous side effects.

Ghost

Overlooked

Cast aside

And I can never

Understand why

Is it that hard to see

What all I bring

If afforded the chance

That never comes

I see so much unhappiness

And by choice, people tend to settle

Which makes me question harder

How can I not be seen?

I am a ghost among the living

Wandering past the blind

Full of potential and a whirlwind energy

Destined to never be unleashed.

Home is You

Rubbing hands together

Trying to keep warm

Surrounded by cold

But feeling like we're home

In each other's arms

Head to head

Lips to lips

Pressed together

We are truly one

We are safe

And secure

A roof of love is high above our heads

With a sturdy foundation of moments beneath

That fostered and grew what we have

What we built

A home, no matter where we are

So long as we are together.

Summer Day

On a summer day

We could drift away

To a world for just us two

Where any problems cannot get through

A sweet little paradise

Where our love booms like an explosive device

There's no rush to get back

Not even once we're swallowed by pitch black

Because how could we leave

Our perfect reprieve?

Planting Seeds

There's a million things I'll come to realize

But never have the words to describe

Though if you give me the time

I can try

Brush the hair from your face

See eye to eye

Because some things I've learned

Are to savor each moment with you, and I hate saying goodbye

An infectious smile

Your soft voice and your laughs,

I hope you stay awhile

While we perfect our crafts

Planting seeds

We can watch them grow

With truth and honesty

And help each other combat the lows

A simple message marks the beginning

Of quite a special journey

That thus far has my head spinning

At the possibilities we can keep churning

Hand in hand

I plead one more kiss

As we step towards new land

That should be full of bliss.

My Princess

A Princess sits up in her tall tower

Looking up it seems endless

But reach her I must

For she needs me

And I find myself here

Because I need the Princess

She may not realize

But we shall save each other

My hero's journey

Is only completed with her courage

And her strength to trust

That I am here to love forever

And here forever to never harm

She has waited far too long

For her Prince

But I am here now

And forever, for you my Princess.

No Doubt

You are perfect for me

So why can't you see

That I'd be perfect for you too

And nothing could be more true

We could be in love and free

Of worry, concern and insecurity

On a path filled with joy and glory

We are the epitome of a love story

Traveling together down life's route

Is our destiny, I have no doubt.

2022

Thoughts from the Mountaintop

Up on the mountaintop

I still lie beneath You

I've put you on such a pedestal

How could I ever reach you?

You are up in the clouds

A Goddess I worship

For nothing in return

And I can't help myself

I look out at this view

And now hope to bring change.

Beauty's Peak

Atop the peak

I can hardly speak

But I know what I think

The sheer beauty is breathtaking

There's a peace and calm

Like when I'm around you

I feel a sense of belonging

That emulates the euphoria

That overcomes me when I hear you laugh

Your smile could match

The warmth of the sun…

If only you were here.

Eerie city

Down below

From above the clouds

It looks desolate

Like I'm alone

And this spot in the world

Is all for me

To search my soul

And know my peace.

Insomnia

Tossing and turning

And nothings working

Because you're not by my side

But I have nothing left to hide

I need to put it all out there

So I can hope to stop living this nightmare.

Taking Time

The clock ticks the same

So remember to slow down

Time takes its toll

And we all pay the piper

So let's steal what we can for now

While we maintain a semblance of control

Pursue passions

They will lead to finding happiness

Just be sure to take the time to look around

Soak in all the surroundings

Until every detail is etched into your head

Take the time to live in the moment

While we have the moment in front of us.

Shadow

I'm the star of the show

Lost in the curtain

Stuck in your shadow

Starting to know nothing for certain

I had my role

And knew my lines

But now it feels I fell down a hole

I missed all the signs

As you overtook me

And left me behind

My blinders were on I couldn't see

How you manipulated my mind

Disrupted my flow

And now I'm just your shadow.

Questioning

Slow, to capture

This fleeting moment

Will it all be a dream?

Or will I reach out and take it,

What I've always wanted

Manifesting in front of my face

Hard to trust

Myself, that it's tangible

Will it not just disappear?

Perhaps there's only one way to find out

But do I have the courage?

I must…I must.

Always Be There

Head down

Lost in thought

Afraid to drown

But twisted in knots

Knowing it shouldn't take much

To turn things around

Yet there seemed to be a lost touch

Something that wouldn't be found

Until finally, fatefully

There shone a light

That could perish the agony

And restore faith right

The timing was elegant

Thus, so was her grace

Natural like the elements

Her beauty defies time and space

There came a smile renewed

Life felt refreshed

It had concocted a new brew

Its ingredients quick to mesh

For one did not save the other

No, simply two came together

Just when they needed one another

To move past the storms once weathered

A hazy gaze

Has become a beaming glow

Previously unsure and stuck in a daze

Now thrilled by the excitement of how high things
may go

One small moment

Came to bear

Time again and again spent

Focused on attention and care

Except it's only the start

To something that could go anywhere

And no matter what, from the heart

I promise to always be there.

Stars

You're a star that shines so brightly

And so I hope to be your shooting star

Something you wish for nightly

Whether near or far

A two way street

That's ready for travel

Once we meet

Could be new and free of hassle

There is luck

And fate

An equation that has struck

Not a second too late

Grateful for each day

With you in my orbit

Here is where we can stay

Building a blinding love bit by bit.

Manifested

Along I came calling

Accustomed to echoes and silence

But quickly I found myself falling

For a smile that's simply timeless

And such sweet words that revive my soul

I'm instilled with newfound hope

My heart feels full

And I can finally breathe again like I'm off the
tightrope

There is what I always wanted

But never thought I would find

Yet I no longer have to feel haunted

Because here you are manifested straight from my mind

The rain can crash down

Nothing else matters to me

As long as you are around

I am oh so excited for what You and I can most assuredly be.

Storm Clouds

There's clouds in the sky

Covering the stars in your eyes

A storm is afoot

And I'm not sure where it's safe to put

My trust

Combating lust

To be what you need

Desperately hoping our love may be freed.

Thank you,

To anyone at all that ever reads this. Earnestly, I cannot properly express my gratitude that you took the time to read some of my words. While there's advice that could be given to not present your poetry chronologically, I want my path to be different. This is my first published work and the start of a new chapter in my life where I can begin focusing more on writing. With that, I wanted to release what I have done that has led me to this point and present it in a raw, honest and transparent way where everybody can quite literally witness the evolution of my writing and thoughts about life and love, and how that has changed and taken shape over my years in college and beyond. I feel like being four years removed from college I have been on a journey to study myself and the world around me, and now I am ready to take steps forwards towards a happy and healthy, fulfilling future. It is imperative we find what we are passionate about and pursue it while we can in this life, and I hope my words may either inspire you or be relatable in some ways. We all share parts of our journey together and again I can't thank you all enough for being a part of mine and supporting me. Until next time, take care!

About the Author

Matthew M Smerglia is a graduate of The Ohio State University where he received his bachelor's degree in consumer and family financial services. *In the Name of Love* is his first published work. He still resides in Columbus post-college but was born and raised in Cleveland with two older brothers. He keeps a busy work schedule and aside from writing, other passions of his include playing several different sports, analyzing and experimenting with a multitude of sports-related statistics, reading, hiking, and having game nights with friends. His adoration and persistence to find "the one" has truly left him a hopelessly hopeless romantic.